Duncan Kidd

Storm Lantern

Salamander Street

PLAYS

Cover image by Katie Innes.

PB ISBN: 9781738429370

10 9 8 7 6 5 4 3 2 1

Further copies of this publication can be purchased from www.salamanderstreet.com

INTRODUCTION

STORM LANTERN—THE FUTURE IS UNWRITTEN

Nominated for a 2023 CATS AWARD for best production
for children and young people

Storm Lantern is the first play commissioned by Strange Town as part of The Future is Unwritten, a three-year programme of new plays for secondary schools, funded by Thrive Edinburgh. The other two are *Her* by Jennifer Adam and *And And And* by Isla Cowan.

These three plays were created to take theatre directly to young people in secondary schools, to kick start conversations and discussion and to pose questions. They are designed to tour and to be of the highest professional standards so that they can be performed in theatres as well as schools.

The first tour of *Storm Lantern* took place between September and October 2022. It toured to 15 secondary schools in Edinburgh and the show was well received by them all.

"You could hear a pin drop in our audience of S3 Drama students" – Craigmount High

For many of the pupils this was the first piece of live theatre they had seen since the lifting of lockdown. Following the shows the cast and myself answered questions from the audience.

The idea for *Storm Lantern* came about because I've always loved an underdog and the story of Hans and Sophie Scholl and a few of their friends standing up to the controlling might of the Nazi party in 1942 Germany fascinated me. I had worked with writer Duncan Kidd before and knew that he, like me, was interested in history and what it tells us about how little things really change. Sadly, it would appear, that we don't learn from history.

We hope that the story of what happened to Sophie, Gisela and Mohr will inspire audiences young and old to learn more about

this relatively recent piece of European history. We should all take heed of Gisela's warning and ensure that something like this never happens again.

Despite the potentially depressing subject matter the rehearsals and the tour were a joy. I'm delighted Duncan's excellent script is being published and I hope you enjoy reading it and use it to discover more about Sophie Scholl and the White Rose movement.

Steve Small
Producer/Director

April 2024

"Storm Lantern was a very atmospheric play which featured superb acting that helped deliver a truly tense production."
- Queensferry High

Storm Lantern first performed on Tuesday 20th Sept 2022 at Craigmount High School, Edinburgh with the following cast:

Robert Mohr:	Rhys Anderson
Gisela Schertling:	Rebeca Forsyth
Sophie Scholl:	Evie Mortimer
Director:	Steve Small
Designer:	Katie Innes
Lighting Designer:	George Cort
Sound Designer:	Gavin Fort
Stage Manager:	Scott Ringan
Deputy Stage Manager:	Magnus Rack
Assistant Director:	Megan Rough

Storm Lantern was written by Duncan Kidd and commissioned and produced by Strange Town. *Storm Lantern* is the first play commissioned by Strange Town as part of 'The Future is Unwritten', a three year programme of new plays for secondary schools, funded by Thrive Edinburgh.

For further information about Strange Town visit www.strangetown.org.uk

THE CAST AND CREATIVES

Gisela Schertling:	**Rebeca Forsyth**
Robert Mohr:	**Paul Beeson**
Sophie Scholl:	**Evie Mortimer**

Director:	**Steve Small**
Designer:	**Katie Innes**
Lighting Designer:	**George Cort**
Sound Designer:	**Gavin Fort**
Production Manager:	**Scott Ringan**
Stage Manager:	**Marisa Ferguson**

ABOUT THE CAST AND CREATIVES

Rebecca Forsyth | Actor *(Gisella Schertling)*

Rebecca played Gisela Schertling in the premiere of *Storm Lantern* in 2022 and has toured extensively with *Antigone Na H'Eireann*, *Women of the Mourning Fields* (Aulos Productions), *The Shakespeares; Scenes From a Marriage* (Storyboard Theatre) and *Balisong* (Strange Town Touring Company and Fast Forward Productions). Other theatre credits include Trojan Barbie (New Celts Productions), *Twelfth Night*, *Men Should Weep* and *The Three Sisters* (Edinburgh Napier University). Screen credits include *The Crown* (Left Bank/Sony/Netflix), *Butterfly* (BFI/Screen Education Edinburgh), *Leekdown* (Strange Town & Media Education) and *The Mouse* (Edinburgh Napier Film Academy)

Paul Beeson | Actor *(Robert Mohr)*

Paul is an actor and writer from Edinburgh. He recently filmed a role in Season 6 of *The Crown* for Netflix. Other credits include Bobby Walker in *Never Trouble Trouble*, Alfie Briggs in *A War of Two Halves*, The Conductor in *The Polar Express*, Will Sussex in *From An Island* and Mr. Pope in *Shark in the Park*.

Paul was part of the BBC Writers Room Scottish Voices in 2020, and has written three award nominated plays, *A War of Two Halves*, *Sweet FA*, and *Never Trouble Trouble*.

In 2022, Paul won a DarkChat award for 'Best Performance in a Play' for his portrayal of Alfie Briggs in *A War of Two Halves*. The play won a further four awards at the same ceremony.

Sweet FA was nominated for 'Best Ensemble' and 'Best Technical Presentation' at the Critics' Awards for Theatre in Scotland 2022.

Evie Mortimer | Actor *(Sophie Scholl)*

Since graduating from the BA Acting and English programme at Edinburgh Napier University, Evie has worked on a number of projects for both stage and screen. Her credits include; *A Midsummer Night's Dream*, (Bard In The Botanics), *Crossing The Void* and *Hysterical*, both written by Sally MacAlister with her company Koi Collective. Evie has also shot two music videos and has several short films in production. Evie is excited to be bringing *Storm Lantern* back to life once more and can't wait to work with the incredible team at Strange Town again.

Duncan Kidd | Writer

Duncan is a writer based in Edinburgh. Since 2007, Duncan's writing has included: *A Field of Our Own*, a commission for NHS Lothian, Strange Town and Hibernian Football Club GameChanger Partnership. A site-specific piece, it was performed underneath the East Stand of Easter Road football stadium during its run at the Edinburgh Festival Fringe 2017.

Being A Dad (Strange Town), based on testimonies of young fathers and prisoners, it was part of the "Year of the Dad" and the Just Festival at the Edinburgh Festival Fringe 2016. It went on to tour Scottish prisons for three years.

Acting Out: A Compact Coriolanus (Charioteer Theatre/Piccolo Teatro). An adaptation of Shakespeare's Coriolanus for 11-14 year olds premiering at Piccolo Teatro, Milan and going on to a national tour of Italy.

Duncan's play *Spoon* was the winner of the Rowan Tree Playwriting Competition.

Duncan's works-in-progress have been supported by Imaginate and performed at Tramway; and as part of the Scottish Mental Health Arts & Film Festival. *Remembering Those* (2018) was performed at Edinburgh Castle for the Armistice centenary, and *A Note Under the Door* (2020) is a digital piece for ThriveFest on World Mental Health Day (2020).

Duncan has worked in participatory projects in community theatre, schools and youth theatre to create and facilitate devised and collaborative work especially with young performers and audiences. Selected work includes: *Trust Me* and *Wasted* (Fast Forward, Strange Town and Rolled Up) (2016 to 2022). Both plays toured schools and *Trust Me* was made into a film and educational resource.

Persevere (2015) was part of the Gretna 100 project, working with a cast of community actors and researchers to devise a promenade performance at Dalmeny Street Drill Hall. This collaboration between Active Inquiry/ Out of the Blue/Strange Town continued with: *Tales of the Hanging Captain* (2016), *The Waves on the Seas* (2017), *The Sideshow* (2019) (Active Inquiry/All or Nothing) and *The Boundary* (2022).

Steve Small | Director/Producer

Steve is the Artistic Director & Joint Executive Director of Strange Town.

Directing credits for Strange Town include: *And And And* by Isla Cowan – Traverse Theatre & Edinburgh schools tour Sept/Oct '23, *Her* by Jennifer Adam – Scottish Storytelling Centre & Edinburgh schools tour Jan/Feb '23, *Storm Lantern* by Duncan Kidd – Scottish Storytelling Centre & Edinburgh schools tour Sept/Oct '22 - nominated for a 2023 CATS award for best production for children and young people, *Balisong* by Jennifer Adam (in partnership with Fast Forward) which toured three times between 2017–2019 with three different casts and performed in every local authority in Scotland; *Dr Korczak's Example* by David Greig first produced for Holocaust Memorial Day 2018 and then at the 2018 & 2019 Edinburgh Festival Fringe and toured secondary schools in Edinburgh, East Lothian and Fife; *A Field of Our Own* by Duncan Kidd – the history of the origins of Hibernian Football club which was the first sold out show of the 2017 Edinburgh Festival Fringe; *Being a Dad* by Duncan Kidd (Fathers' Network Scotland), 2016 Edinburgh Festival Fringe sell out and toured to prisons, community centres and conferences.

Previously Steve was Associate Director, Dundee Rep, Head of Education, Royal Lyceum Theatre, Edinburgh and Associate Director, Scottish Youth Theatre.

Katie Innes | Designer

Katie Innes graduated with a BA (hons) Drama and Performance degree from Queen Margaret University, specialising in design and scenic art, further developing her skills on the Scenehouse Design course. As the Design and Production Manager for Strange Town, she works regularly on their youth theatre productions including, during the pandemic, a large-scale, multi-media event *Gen Z: The Future is Unwritten*. For the touring company she designed the set and costumes for; *Dr Korczak's Example* by David Greig, *Storm Lantern* by Duncan Kidd, *Her* by Jennifer Adam and *And And And* by Isla Cowan. It is Katie's hope that having a motivated, creative working mum will be an inspiration to her daughters.

George Cort | Lighting designer

George Cort has been a professional theatre lighting technician and designer for over 15 years. During that time he has lit dance, musical theatre, opera and drama. Recent credits for Strange Town touring company include *Storm Lantern*, *Her*, *And And And* , Strange Town's summer youth theatre shows at the Traverse Theatre as well as *The Gods, The Gods, The Gods*, for Wright & Grainger at the Edinburgh Festival Fringe 2022.

Gavin Fort | Sound designer

Gavin is a sound recordist, engineer, producer and tutor. After studying Popular Music at Edinburgh Napier University, he went on to complete an MSc in Sound Design at The University of Edinburgh. He has worked on a wide range of projects both in and out of the studio from albums to film shoots to wildlife recording.

Scott Ringan | Production Manager

Scott is an Edinburgh-based Stage Manager working most recently with the Tron Theatre, Glasgow, on *Escaped Alone*. He worked on the 2022 revival of *The Strange Undoing of Prudencia Hart* at the Edinburgh Fringe Festival and then toured America with the production in 2023 prior to an eight week Off-Broadway engagement. Other work includes: *Peter Pan* (Crossroads Pantomimes), *And And And* (Strange Town), *Thrown* (National Theatre of Scotland), *Sean and Daro Flake It 'Til They Make It* (Traverse Theatre) and *Sinbad* (Brunton Theatre). Scott is delighted to be back working on *Storm Lantern* after its successful first tour in 2022 and to be Production Manager for the Strange Town Touring Company for this revival.

Marisa Ferguson | Stage manager

Marisa has a BA(Hons) Degree in Technical Theatre from Rose Bruford College and has worked in professional Stage Management, in a wide range of productions, for over 20 years. Theatre credits include: West Yorkshire/Leeds Playhouse, Northern Stage, Northern Ballet Theatre, Royal Shakespeare Company, Royal Exchange Theatre–Manchester, Fiery Angel, Scottish Opera, Scamp Theatre Company, Watford Palace Theatre, Visible Fictions, Magnetic North, and Royal Lyceum Theatre–Edinburgh.

Duncan Kidd

Storm Lantern

CHARACTERS

GISELA

MOHR
(plainclothes Secret State Policeman: Gestapo)

SOPHIE

SCENE ONE

1960s.

GISELA is delivering a lecture on the dangers of National Socialism to local students. She has her notes in a suitcase—she is nervous—she takes out the leaflets—drops them —pushes them back together.

GISELA: Sorry excuse me. Just a moment.

I..

Um..

(She finds her place)

"It is unbelievable to what extent you must deceive a people in order to rule it..." Hitler said. Or he might have said, "Betray. Betray a people in order to rule it." They founded a ministry of propaganda just to do so. Goebbels said...

...

Let's get this out of the way, OK?
I want you to know something.

(She doesn't say it)

I am not looking for your forgiveness. I am not looking for your pity. Or even your condemnation

I am here to give you a warning.

I...

GISELA drops her notes, they scatter, she tries to pick them up, but they are in a different order.

SCENE TWO

MOHR is a plainclothes Secret State Policeman (Gestapo).
SOPHIE and GISELA are in separate cells.
A stack of white leaflets.
HANS SCHOLL is out of sight, absent but present.

MOHR: I want you to tell the truth. The whole, complete truth down to the last detail. Only the truth, understand? Is that clear?

GISELA: Yes. Yes. Of course. Yes. The truth. The truth. Yes, of course. I'll tell you the truth. Yes, of course. Please.

SOPHIE: The truth?

MOHR: Yes.

SOPHIE: You are interested in the truth?

MOHR: Yes, of course.

SOPHIE: Since when?

MOHR: What?

SOPHIE: That's interesting that's all.

MOHR: Do you swear? The truth, and nothing else?

SOPHIE: As best I can.

MOHR: We'll start with the easy stuff shall we? Name?

GISELA: Gisela Schertling.

SOPHIE: Sophie Scholl.

MOHR: Age?

GISELA: 21.

SOPHIE: 21.

MOHR: Occupation?

GISELA: Student.

SOPHIE: Student.

3

MOHR: Where do you live?

GISELA: Munich.

SOPHIE: Munich.

MOHR: Are your parents of German blood?

BOTH: Yes.

MOHR: Are your grandparents of German blood?

BOTH: Yes.

MOHR: Father's occupation?

SOPHIE: Business Adviser.

GISELA: Owner of a printing press.

MOHR: Are you a member of the Nazi Party?

BOTH: No.

MOHR: (*Holds up a leaflet*) Now, have you seen this before?

"To all students. To the youth of Germany".

This morning someone distributed thousands of these at the university. (*He reads over it—paraphrasing*) The Nazis have drugged and duped the youth of this country with their mindless propaganda and empty slogans. Trained them to be conscienceless executioners and blind, stupid followers of the Führer. Students! The German people look to us. We must smash Hitler's wicked regime and restore Germany's freedom and honour and blah, blah, blah, etc., etc., so on and so forth. Sound familiar? Any ideas where these leaflets might have come from?

Both shrug.

SCENE THREE

MOHR interviews SOPHIE.

SOPHIE: Will this take long?

MOHR: It will take as long as it takes. Do you have some where better to be, Miss Scholl?

SOPHIE: I'm supposed to be getting the train just after six, I'm going home for the weekend.

MOHR: Let's see what we can do. Could you tell me, in your own words, what you did today? And the truth, remember, please.

SOPHIE: Well, I got up and I had some tea and Gisela, that's my friend...

MOHR: Gisela Schertling?

SOPHIE: Yes.

MOHR: Do you know a lot of other people in Munich?

SOPHIE: Not really. Just Gisela. And my brother.

MOHR: Sorry to interrupt. Carry on, please.

SOPHIE: And Gisela and I said we'd meet up for lunch but then decided to go and see my Mum and Dad for the weekend instead, like I just said, and I said to Hans...

MOHR: Your brother?

SOPHIE: Yes. I said we just need to go by the university and tell Gisela what I'm doing, because I won't be having lunch with her now obviously. And when we got there everyone was just leaving class and I noticed these leaflets, piles of them, about this high, lying on the marble balcony way up high above everyone, you know above the atrium, and as I walked by I gave them a little shove—so they fluttered —just fluttered in the air—as everyone came out of class—and they landed all down on top of everybody.

MOHR: Why did you do that?

SOPHIE: I don't know. I just felt like it. In that moment. I wish I hadn't. It was stupid. Then the janitor's running towards me and he's grabbing me by the arm and he's shouting "you are under arrest" over and over again.

MOHR: So that was silly OK, yes. And the janitor was maybe a little overzealous. I know the type. Probably just keen to claim a reward? He hasn't helped things, causing a fuss. But you do see that it looks like you and your brother took these leaflets in your suitcase and put them there yourselves?

SOPHIE: Yes, I can see it looks like that.

MOHR: I know, I know. Can you think of anything, did you see anything, anything at all that might help point to who did leave them?

SOPHIE: No. No nothing.

MOHR: You're sure. It could just be the smallest thing?

SOPHIE: Sorry no. I didn't notice anything after I pushed the leaflets, I was being arrested.

MOHR: Yes. I see. Just some other questions. Have you bought any postage stamps recently?

SOPHIE: What?

MOHR: Who carried the suitcase?

SOPHIE: My brother.

MOHR: Was it heavy?

SOPHIE: No, it was empty

MOHR: How many stamps did you buy?

SOPHIE: 20-25?

MOHR: Do you have any left?

SOPHIE: No.

6

MOHR: You live with your brother?

SOPHIE: Hans, yes.

MOHR: Why would you have an empty suitcase?

SOPHIE: I was going home to see my parents. I was going to pick up some clean clothes they had washed for me.

MOHR: Have you ever seen these leaflets before?

SOPHIE: Not before this morning.

MOHR: No?

SOPHIE: No, never.

MOHR: OK. Thank you for your cooperation, Sophie.

SOPHIE: You're welcome.

MOHR: Don't worry. If you're lucky, we'll get you to that train after all.

SCENE FOUR

GISELA and SOPHIE enter, separately. They are back from holiday and both carrying suitcases. GISELA is joining SOPHIE at university for the first time.

GISELA: It's so good to see you, Sophie. I've missed you.

SOPHIE: Welcome to Munich.

GISELA picks up SOPHIE's suitcase.

GISELA: God, what's in that? Books?!

SOPHIE: Don't start.

GISELA: Too much reading rots your brain, you know.

SOPHIE: What?

GISELA: You're lucky I've arrived. You might actually start having some fun.

SOPHIE: I have fun...

GISELA: Yeah, when I'm around. To force you to actually join in with things!

GISELA starts to exit.

SOPHIE picks up a leaflet that is lying on the ground.

SOPHIE: (*Shouting*) Gisela. Look at this!

GISELA: Shh. Sophie. Be quiet. You will get us in trouble.

SOPHIE hands her the leaflet.

GISELA: Where did you get this?

SOPHIE: Someone left it here. I just picked it up.

GISELA: Do you think we should report it?

SOPHIE: What? Why?

GISELA: It is treason.

SOPHIE: It is the truth.

GISELA: Put it back. It's got nothing to do with us. Sophie, put it away. Get rid of that thing before they catch you with it.

SOPHIE: Alright. Come on, you've got to meet Hans.

GISELA: He's only going to be disappointing, the way you've built him up!

SOPHIE: No, no. You'll love him. Everybody does.

GISELA: Is he good looking?

SOPHIE: He's my brother.

GISELA: Well, is he?

SOPHIE: Find out for yourself. It'll be nice to break up the boys club at uni. We've got to stick together. They outnumber us 10 to 1.

They exit.

SCENE FIVE

MOHR interviews GISELA.

GISELA sits staring ahead. Terrified.

MOHR: Please, relax. It is just a few questions.

GISELA: I didn't do anything. I promise you, please. I don't know anything. Please.

MOHR: I just want to ask you about Sophie.

GISELA relaxes slightly.

GISELA: OK?

MOHR: How long have you known her?

GISELA: A couple of years. We did National Labour service together. We were all on a farm by the sea, there were lots of us, but I was the only one Sophie really got on with, the others were too...

MOHR: Too what?

GISELA: Just... she didn't get on with them so well. Noisy, too noisy for her.

MOHR: You are still good friends?

GISELA: Yes.

MOHR: And Hans? Boyfriend?

GISELA: No.

MOHR: No?

GISELA: Maybe he sees it like that, I don't know. We are just friends.

MOHR: And what happened today?

GISELA: Today?

MOHR: You know that treasonous leaflets were distributed at the university?

GISELA: Oh, yes. I saw big piles of them stacked up outside the door when I came out of my class and scattered all about on the ground. But I didn't really think about them that much because I had to go.

MOHR: Go where?

GISELA: I was supposed to be having lunch with Sophie.

MOHR: She didn't tell you she was going somewhere else instead?

GISELA: I didn't see her.

MOHR: She wasn't in class today?

GISELA: No, and neither was Hans actually. I went to look for them at the flat and then when I got there, there were policemen there, and they arrested me. But I didn't do anything, I swear.

MOHR: Why do you think they arrested you?

GISELA: I don't know. I thought that Sophie and Hans must have been arrested too. I thought maybe it was to do with the leaflets.

MOHR: What? Why did you think that?

GISELA: I didn't, I mean... because of the things they say sometimes. The things they talk about.

MOHR: What do you mean? Do you mean like things written in the leaflets?

GISELA: Yes.

MOHR: You have heard them say treasonous, traitorous things?

GISELA: Yes.

MOHR: Have you ever seen them making the leaflets? Leaving them somewhere? Posting them?

GISELA: No, never. No nothing like that. Ever. No. No. I've never seen anything like that.

MOHR: But you think the leaflets might be written by them?

GISELA: Yes, definitely. Definitely they could be.

MOHR: Thank you, Gisela. I know it is not always easy to do your duty. You have done well. Your loyalty will be appreciated.

SCENE SIX

Outside. The street, near the Post Office.
SOPHIE is standing, alone, putting a stamp on an envelope.
GISELA enters, holding a couple of large sheets of stamps.

GISELA: Got them.

SOPHIE: Thank you. You're a lifesaver.

GISELA: Why couldn't you get them?

SOPHIE: I've already got lots. Couldn't get too many, it'd look suspicious.

GISELA: It is suspicious! The man in the Post Office gave me a funny look. What are you going to do with them all?

SOPHIE: I've got a lot of writing to do.

GISELA: Clearly.

SOPHIE holds out several A4 envelopes.

SOPHIE: And now you can help me post some.

GISELA: What are they?

SOPHIE: Love letters.

GISELA: How many men have you got on the go? Does Fritz know?

SOPHIE: It's not like that, quite. Now, they must all be posted from different post boxes.

GISELA: What? Why?

SOPHIE: So, it seems like they've all been posted by different people.

GISELA: You do make me do the strangest things.

SOPHIE: Post this will you?

GISELA trying to read the name and address on the envelope.

GISELA: Who does that say? Do I know him? I bet I do.

SOPHIE: Come on.

They exit.

SCENE SEVEN

MOHR interviews SOPHIE.

The evidence from the flat has been brought to headquarters, and MOHR has been genuinely surprised, even shocked to realise Sophie is guilty, but he is trying to hide it.

SOPHIE yawns.

MOHR: Would you like some coffee? It might help keep you awake?

SOPHIE: What time is it?

MOHR: 3am.

SOPHIE: No, thank you.

MOHR: We will be here for a while yet. As long as it takes? It's real coffee, by the way.

SOPHIE: Real coffee? No one's been able to get that for years?

MOHR: For most people the shortages are very bad, yes. But you are a special case now, aren't you? A Very Important Person. Would you like some?

SOPHIE nods guiltily.

MOHR gets her some coffee.

SOPHIE: Thank you.

They sit in silence for a while as SOPHIE drinks her coffee.

SOPHIE: Do you know this one? So, the first man says "Do you hear they have arrested Robert?", the second goes, "why? He is a good man. He has done nothing wrong!" The first man says "Yes, exactly! That's why!"

MOHR: Yes, I've heard that one. A joke like that could get you in trouble, you know?

SOPHIE: ...

MOHR: The Ministry of Propaganda has said that every German must be honest, intelligent and a National Socialist. "That's impossible," says the woman. "Why?" says the man. "If they are intelligent and a Nazi," says the woman "they are not honest. If they are honest and a Nazi, they are not intelligent. And if they are intelligent and honest, they are not a Nazi."

SOPHIE laughs in agreement.

MOHR: (*not smiling*) You find that funny?

SOPHIE: I find it true.

MOHR: You admit to being anti-Nazi?

SOPHIE: That's not so unusual?

MOHR: Isn't it?

SOPHIE: It doesn't make me guilty.

MOHR: This afternoon I thought you would be free by now. I really did. You seemed so calm. So innocent. Maybe it was all just a coincidence. This girl sitting here wouldn't do something so stupid. Really, I am too naïve, too trusting, that's my problem.

SOPHIE: You still haven't found who you are looking for then?

MOHR: We have found plenty of things. We have been to your apartment, Sophie. What do you think we might have found?

SOPHIE: I've no idea.

MOHR has a bundle of things found at the flat: papers, leaflets, stamps, books, and the suitcase. He looks through them. Picks things out.

MOHR: "Storm Lantern" what is that?

SOPHIE: A magazine. We published it just for ourselves.

MOHR: Do I need to be worried about what I might read?

SOPHIE: No.

MOHR: What is this name? A Nazi name?

SOPHIE: The lantern shows the way out of the storm. The storm dies.

MOHR: Lanterns go out, Sophie. When the storm is too strong. White Rose. Storm Lantern. The names, like the contents, are too flowery and pretentious. For me. That's just my opinion.

SOPHIE: Is it?

MOHR: Who do you think you will reach? You are not going to talk to normal people like this. Real people. You need red meat propaganda. Short, sharp, punchy. You need pictures, sounds, radio, television, film. Not schoolgirl essays.

Picks up a copy of St Joan.

MOHR: St Joan?

SOPHIE: Have you read it?

MOHR: She tried to lead France to freedom and died a martyr's death?

SOPHIE: At the hands of her petty-minded captors...

MOHR: You see yourself as Joan, Sophie?

SOPHIE: ...

MOHR: You know the Führer has a copy too? Perhaps he sees himself as Joan? A little commoner—what does your leaflet call him? The Austrian Corporal—who's put on his crusading armour to take on the whole established order of Europe and topple it on its arse?

SOPHIE: Maybe that's how he likes to look on his posters but if that's how he sees it he is the Devil's Saint not God's.

MOHR: Was Joan God's Saint?

SOPHIE: Of course.

MOHR: Not just an ordinary girl, a misguided girl, called upon, heard voices telling her, to do something extraordinary in the name of what, she thought, was right?

SOPHIE: And harassed by cynical men who hid their moral cowardice behind "realism" and "experience"?

MOHR: Clearly, I should leave these sorts of discussions to you very clever students shouldn't I? What am I? Just a policeman.

He fits the leaflets into the suitcase. The number of leaflets fit the suitcase exactly.

MOHR: Fits?

SOPHIE: Neat.

MOHR: Perfectly. Coincidence, isn't it?

SOPHIE: Isn't it?

MOHR holds up several sheets of stamps.

MOHR: That's a lot of stamps.

SOPHIE: I write a lot of letters.

MOHR: Please.

SOPHIE: ...

MOHR: Your brother has confessed everything, Sophie.

SOPHIE: He can't have, there is nothing to confess. And even if there was, he wouldn't.

MOHR: You know they sent me specially? Came all the way down from Berlin. To find you. Imagine that. Here I've been for weeks, searching high and low, for these troublemakers, and what was I looking for? Well, it wasn't you.

SOPHIE is suddenly fidgety, restless.

MOHR: What's wrong?

SOPHIE: You use torture? I've heard that. Beating, even killing someone to get a confession?

MOHR: You think I'm going to do that?

SOPHIE: No. I am not worried about me. Hans.

MOHR: The Gestapo doesn't torture people! I don't know where you've heard that. Come on look, where are the thumbscrews and torture-racks? It's just paperclips and coffee cups? You don't believe me? I promise, you can see Hans, and see him as much as you like if that would reassure you.

SOPHIE: Yes.

MOHR: We will go and see him when we've finished. Shortly. He is absolutely fine, don't worry. He and the others are just, voluntarily, telling us some very valuable things as we speak, very valuable. So, you don't need to hide anything from me anymore. Maybe that might be a relief?

SOPHIE: What others?

MOHR: This you didn't hear? Now, who have we brought in? Gisela, Alex, Christoph?

SOPHIE is genuinely shocked, her composure gone for the first time.

SOPHIE: Christoph?

MOHR: He has two little children? Is that right?

SOPHIE: Three.

MOHR: Three, sorry. My mistake.

SOPHIE: He has nothing to do with this. None of them do.

MOHR: No? It seems quite a little conspiracy, this "White Rose" of yours? Or is it the "German Resistance" now? That must be a crowd. With a big, official name like that?

SOPHIE: No. No. They have nothing to do with it.

MOHR: No? That's not what they are telling us.

SOPHIE: It's not true. (*pointing to all the evidence*) You're right.

MOHR: I know.

SOPHIE: But Hans and I wrote the leaflets. We did.

MOHR: Just the two of you?

SOPHIE: Yes, and we took them to the university this morning, I mean yesterday morning, in the suitcase and we stacked and scattered them there, threw them off the balcony and left them there for everyone to read. That's the truth.

MOHR: You realise what you are admitting to?

SOPHIE: Yes.

MOHR: And you managed to keep this covered up, kept it hidden from everyone around you?

SOPHIE: I mean maybe one or two people, friends, heard us talk. But we didn't get anyone involved. It would have been too dangerous.

MOHR: Yes, yes it would have been.

SOPHIE: So, we didn't.

MOHR: I see what you are trying to do here, Sophie. It is noble, but...

SOPHIE: I'm not trying to do anything. Just to tell the truth. You are right, it is a relief.

17

MOHR: This was more than a few leaflets thrown about in a panic. For months and months. Town to town. The leaflets cropping up again and again. You don't expect me to believe it was only two of you?

SOPHIE: We used to laugh. Hans and I. We'd laugh at you. When we were posting leaflets from different places or taking trains to different towns. Making you think we were some huge organisation, that covered the country. We laughed at how confused you must be. How you must be getting really worried.

MOHR: You thought you could outwit us?

SOPHIE: We did for a while, didn't we?

MOHR: Yes, you did.

Trying to reassert her composure.

SOPHIE: Do you know this one? So, Hitler says to Goebbels...

MOHR: No. No. Thank you. Sophie. That's enough for just now. You look exhausted. You should get some rest.

SCENE EIGHT

The Apartment.
GISELA finishes reading a letter, that has been left lying around. She puts it down and starts packing a suitcase with clothes.
SOPHIE enters.

SOPHIE: What are you doing?

GISELA: I'm sending warm clothes to the Front. (*Pointing to letter*) Like Fritz asked you to?

SOPHIE: He's my boyfriend.

GISELA: I know.

SOPHIE: No.

GISELA: Why not?

SOPHIE: I won't do anything which makes this war last even a minute longer.

GISELA: You won't help at all?

SOPHIE: No.

GISELA: And if they freeze?

SOPHIE: The war must end.

GISELA: Everything is so straightforward for you, Sophie.

SOPHIE: This is straightforward. We are wrong and we must be stopped. Fritz knows this, I've talked to him about it, he's even beginning to agree.

GISELA: Whatever you think of the leaders...

SOPHIE: We are led by criminals.

GISELA: It is Fritz. Out there in Russia. Freezing in the snow.

SOPHIE: I know.

GISELA: You cannot be argued with!

SOPHIE: My mum's friend is a nurse. They came to her orphanage. In their black vans. They came for the disabled children. They had told them they were going on a trip.

GISELA: No, Sophie I don't want to know this.

SOPHIE: They went into to the vans and they never came back.

GISELA: No...

SOPHIE: She saw it herself. The other children, the ones from outside, they chant "here come the murder boxes". They know, and you don't? Our own propaganda celebrates it—it's for their own good, it's for everybody's good, they are just "useless eaters".

GISELA: It's too much, it's too much to take in, can't we talk about something else?

SOPHIE: No. This is what you support.

GISELA: Anything else, please? We should just...

SOPHIE: And if you didn't know, you do now—I am telling you. My mother's friend she saw it herself. Hans, Alex they have seen other things, worse things in the army in Poland, in Russia.

GISELA: They've heard it, yes. That's enemy propaganda. It's lies, Sophie.

SOPHIE: They've seen it. It is happening. And you know it.

GISELA: I don't know it. I don't know it at all. We, we should just keep our heads down, until it's over, that's safest, that's best isn't it?

SOPHIE: No, it isn't.

SCENE NINE

MOHR interviews GISELA.

MOHR: Well, I don't think either of us expected to see each other again so soon?

GISELA: No.

MOHR: Have you been telling the whole truth, Gisela?

GISELA: Yes.

MOHR: I don't think so. You were friends with Sophie, yes? You have told me that. But you and Hans? I think you are much closer to them both than you have been letting on. You were with them both nearly every day. You stayed with them. You ate meals with them. In their flat. Wouldn't just feel better to tell the truth? All of it? Not hide anything?

GISELA: Yes. Yes. Of course.

MOHR: You agree?

GISELA: Yes.

MOHR: If you were to say, what do you think, just a rough number now. How many times have you and Hans had sex?

GISELA: What?

MOHR: It's OK. Just answer the question. Please.

GISELA: We... we haven't.

MOHR: You slept there, in Hans's room?

GISELA: Yes. Once, yes. It was too late to go home. But Hans slept on the floor.

MOHR: Gisela, I thought we weren't hiding anything anymore? I know this is a difficult subject to talk about, but I am not here to judge you, just to find out what happened. Please, it's OK, what would you like me to call it? You slept together. In Hans's room.

GISELA: No, we didn't. We only... only at my place.

MOHR: Let me get to the point. You saw Sophie every day, you stayed in Hans's room many, many times? And you never saw a leaflet? Never saw any equipment for making leaflets?

GISELA: No.

MOHR: How can that be?

GISELA: They must have been hidden somewhere.

MOHR: Thousands and thousands of leaflets? Hand printed on a giant printing machine? Leaflets spread all across Germany? Industrial quantities of ink and paper. A plot to overthrow the Party and end the war, all carried out from a room you often slept in and led by a man you were sleeping with? And you are telling me you never once saw any evidence? Any evidence at all?

GISELA: No.

MOHR: Gisela, how can you expect me to believe you?

GISELA: I...

MOHR: It is not plausible. Not even slightly.

GISELA: No.

MOHR: It is OK, Gisela, it is OK. Just tell the truth. It will be much, much better for you. Trust me.

GISELA: In the last few days, before we were arrested, I thought, I thought maybe something was going on.

MOHR: Yes? Go on.

GISELA: They were working very hard in Hans's room. Day and night.

MOHR: What were they doing?

GISELA: They said they were studying. For the exams coming up.

MOHR: Printing machines make a noise. Loud enough to hear from another room.

GISELA: I don't know. I've never seen one. Or heard one before.

MOHR: Your father is a printer, Gisela, don't tell me you don't know. Where were you?

GISELA: In Sophie's room.

MOHR: Doing what?

GISELA: I don't know. Just reading.

MOHR: You didn't go into the other room? At all?

GISELA: No.

MOHR: Gisela.

GISELA: I didn't because I didn't want to. I didn't want to see. I didn't want to know what they were doing. And they didn't want me to know either.

MOHR: Why?

GISELA: I thought that maybe they were doing something they shouldn't be. Something illegal.

MOHR: You knew what they were doing.

GISELA: It was too obvious. They couldn't hide it, not really. They were getting careless I think, they weren't really trying to hide it anymore. Yes, I knew.

MOHR: Thank you, Gisela.

SCENE TEN

The Apartment.

A stack of white leaflets. A book left open with passages underlined.

GISELA reads a leaflet.

GISELA picks up the book and starts looking at some of the things that have been underlined, she notices something and takes out the leaflet and compares the two. They are the same passage—quotes from these books have been used in the leaflet.

SOPHIE enters.

SOPHIE: Gisela, what are you doing?

GISELA holds up the leaflet.

GISELA: This...

SOPHIE closes all the books and tidies things away.

SOPHIE: Probably best to mind your own business. For your own sake.

GISELA: This is you, isn't it? This is what you and Hans and the others have been doing?

SOPHIE: I don't know what you are talking about and even if I did, talking about it would be very dangerous for whoever did have something to do with it.

GISELA: You!

SOPHIE: Gisela!

GISELA: Sophie. What if you are caught?

SOPHIE: Then we won't be caught.

GISELA: You can't be sure. Someone might tell on you.

SOPHIE: Who?

GISELA: Anyone. And then they will kill you.

SOPHIE: No. No. We cannot afford to be killed. We need to survive. There is a better future—that starts with these.

GISELA: And if they do catch you?

SOPHIE: Then I'm ready.

GISELA: What?

SOPHIE: So many people are dying for this stupid war, it's time someone stood up and died against it.

GISELA: What? Sophie, what are you saying?

SOPHIE: Someone has to do what is right.

GISELA: If the only way to be "right" or "good" in this country is to die, I don't want to be "right" or "good". I just want to live.

SOPHIE: It's only a matter of time before they find us. And then these leaflets won't be enough.

GISELA: No, Sophie, please, no. What are you going to do?

SOPHIE: I don't know yet.

GISELA: Sophie. Please. Don't do something stupid. Or you'll get us all killed.

SOPHIE: Just don't say anything.

GISELA: I won't, Sophie. I wouldn't. I just...

SOPHIE: Say nothing. If they capture any of us. The rest of us have agreed already. Anything the Gestapo know already just agree with it, but don't add anything. Don't tell them anything they don't already know. Just say as little as possible. If you can, say nothing.

SCENE ELEVEN

MOHR interviews GISELA.

MOHR: You have impeccable credentials, Gisela. Your politics are spotless. You were in the Hitler Youth. Your father runs a press printing good Nazi propaganda. Your parents are both party members. Where did it go wrong?

GISELA: I've tried to help. I promise.

MOHR: But you knew and you didn't tell anyone? Sophie's father is in prison because his secretary heard him muttering about the Führer. Neighbours have got neighbours sent to camps because their dog barks too loudly. Kids snitch on their teachers. And you, Gisela, a loyal Nazi, discover a genuine plot to overthrow the Party and you say nothing?

GISELA: I didn't have time to, it all happened so fast.

MOHR: When did you find out?

GISELA: You know, like I said. A few days before we were arrested. Before the leaflets at the university? It all happened so fast, I didn't know what was happening.

MOHR: Did you try and stop them?

GISELA: No, I couldn't. It would have been pointless. It would have made no difference. They wouldn't have listened to me. They were going to do it whatever I did or said.

MOHR: So, you just went along with it?

GISELA: I had to whether I wanted to or not.

MOHR: Why?

GISELA: You don't understand. You don't understand how persuasive he was. I can't explain it, he kept manipulating me. He was the first, my first. He promised to marry me. But then I felt trapped. I tried to get out. He threatened to kill himself if I said I would leave. But then he was so charming again, made it all make sense. It's like he was in control of me. I think I was under a spell. Really.

MOHR: You were in love with him?

GISELA: No. I don't know. It's not just that. He has this effect on lots of people. He has this charisma. He likes to be the leader. To have a group of people hang on his every word.

Sophie too, they are so clever, they can tie you up with words, even when you know what they are saying is wrong.

MOHR: You know what they were saying was wrong?

GISELA: Yes. But I was with them so much, I didn't have any time to think for myself.

MOHR: You could have spent less time with them?

GISELA: No, I tried but I... it was like I was being made into something I was not, becoming like them.

MOHR: You agreed with them?

GISELA: They made me doubt. I'm sorry.

MOHR: What did they make you doubt?

GISELA: The war. The Party. Everything. They made me think that it was all wrong. I even thought, I even doubted the Führer. I'm sorry. Please, believe me. I'm sorry.

MOHR: Did you help them? Did you help print the leaflets yourself?

GISELA: No.

MOHR: Did you mail the leaflets?

GISELA: Yes. Once. I helped Sophie mail some.

MOHR: Did Sophie tell you what was in them?

GISELA: No. But I knew. Really, I knew.

MOHR: Gisela. You didn't go to the flat for lunch that day? You went to tell the others Hans and Sophie had been arrested. You went to warn them? So, they could get away?

GISELA: Yes.

MOHR: But you met the police there instead?

GISELA: Yes.

MOHR: Did you not think? Did you not realise how dangerous this all was?

GISELA: Yes. But it was like it was happening to someone else. It was like it just had to happen, it had to take its own course, there was nothing I could do. I don't know. It seems like a dream.

MOHR: They are dangerous people, Gisela.

GISELA: I know.

MOHR: And they have made you their victim.

GISELA: Yes, yes, that's right.

MOHR: The court will see that.

GISELA: Do you think so?

MOHR: They will see you were taken in, they will see you only had a few days to wrestle between what you thought was love and your duty to the Fatherland.

GISELA: Yes, that's right.

MOHR: Do you accept that you have made a terrible mistake?

GISELA: I do.

MOHR: You admit you wavered from the National cause?

GISELA: Yes.

MOHR: Do you want to make amends for what you have done?

GISELA: Yes.

MOHR: This will all be over soon, don't worry. Do you want to be accepted back into the National People's Community?

GISELA: Yes. I will do my best. I will work hard. I want to help the war. I could work in a factory. I could make bombs. Please. I will do anything.

MOHR: Do you want to live as a good German woman and a model Nazi citizen?

GISELA: Yes.

MOHR: Gisela. I want you to write down the names of every person you saw at the flat. Every name of someone you think might be involved with this plot and these leaflets.

GISELA takes the paper and starts writing.

SCENE TWELVE

MOHR interviews SOPHIE.

SOPHIE has slept, and has slept well, she is better rested. MOHR has not. He is eating a sandwich.

MOHR: Sleep well?

SOPHIE: Yes, thank you.

MOHR: Have you eaten?

SOPHIE: No.

MOHR: Please.

MOHR gives her half of his sandwich and an orange.

SOPHIE: Thank you.

MOHR: You're welcome.

SOPHIE: My brother gave chocolate to a prisoner in Poland.

MOHR: That was kind of him.

SOPHIE: Do you think his kindness mattered when he was part of the army that put her there?

MOHR: Well, maybe it made him feel better. How are you enjoying you enjoying your cell?

SOPHIE: It's nice, thank you.

MOHR: Isn't it? Big window, fresh sheets, a friendly cellmate to talk to. It's all been rolled out for you. You're a very...

SOPHIE: Does that mean that've we've got to you?

MOHR: Big names in the Party have shared that cell. You should be proud.

SOPHIE: You see. The Nazis even turn on each other. This system destroys trust and loyalty and...

MOHR: Yes, I've read your leaflets. I've been enjoying our chats, Sophie. But now that you've had some proper time to rest, to think about the things we've talked about... the things that I've explained to you. You must have realised now the problem is with the way you've been brought up? Your beliefs have been warped.

SOPHIE: No.

MOHR: Everyone here admires you.

SOPHIE: ...

MOHR: Your courage. Your self-possession. Your self-sacrifice. Your willingness to take the blame to save others.

SOPHIE: ...

MOHR: It's just a pity you've used it all against your own country. Against your own people.

SOPHIE: Everything I've done has been for my country, for my people.

MOHR: How can you think that? When you'll happily threaten the war effort? If the war turns against us, then it will be our turn to be invaded.

SOPHIE: Good.

MOHR: What?

SOPHIE: I hope we are invaded. And soon. Someone needs to come and liberate us.

MOHR: You can't say that. No one should be allowed to say things like that.

SOPHIE: People should be allowed to say what they like.

MOHR: There are limits, of decency and good taste.

SOPHIE: You know, many people think like us. They are just too scared to speak out. Somebody had to make a start, to show that it was possible.

MOHR: You think so?

SOPHIE: People are ready to rise up.

MOHR: No, they are not. Do you not think I would know? It's my job to track these things. It's you. You are the resistance. You and your friends.

SOPHIE: No, there are more, many more.

MOHR: Oh really? Who else? Any names? No?

SOPHIE: No.

MOHR: You understand the Leader and the country are one? The Leader is the country, the country is the Leader. If you betray the leader, you betray the people. So don't tell me you did it for the people.

SOPHIE: You believe that nonsense? Since I was little, everything, schools, sports, clubs, newspapers, radio—everything you see, everything you read, everything you hear has been in one voice. Yours. And it has all been a lie.

MOHR: So, all we needed was a little of your propaganda to set us right?

SOPHIE: There might be two propagandas. But there is only one truth.

MOHR: Well, it depends...

SOPHIE: Either two hundred thousand German soldiers are dead at Stalingrad. Or they're not. Either we are losing this war, or we aren't. Either we killed those children, are killing the Poles, are murdering the Jews. Or we aren't? Well, are we?

MOHR: That's outside of my department.

SOPHIE: Is it?

MOHR: I'm not getting into discussions about other...

SOPHIE: What will you say?

MOHR: When?

SOPHIE: When they come to you ask you what you did to stop it?

MOHR: I'm not the one under questioning here.

SOPHIE: No. Not yet.

MOHR: I don't need to answer to you.

SOPHIE: You've lived with the lies for so long it's not that you can't see the truth anymore. It's that you don't even know what truth is. It is not me with warped beliefs, it's you.

MOHR almost ends the interview.

MOHR: Why did you go to the university, Hans and you? All that careful work, covering your tracks, keeping us fooled, and you did, I admit it, and then you go and do that, in broad daylight, in a place full of people who know who you are? Why did you take that risk? Did you want to die?

SOPHIE: No.

MOHR: Did Hans? In these last few days. He's changed hasn't he? He's become paranoid. He thought someone was on to you? Who?

SOPHIE: I don't know what you're talking about.

MOHR: You told me you only knew Hans and Gisela in Munich? The safe names to give me. Christoph, Alex... How many of you are there really?

SOPHIE: I've told you. It was me and my brother. Alone.

MOHR: How will they feel about Hans making a "statement" like that? Putting their lives at risk too? Not just yours.

SOPHIE: I know what you're doing.

MOHR: Your brother is a dangerous person.

SOPHIE: You think so?

MOHR: I know it wasn't you, Sophie. Not really...

SOPHIE: No?

MOHR: He was the leader, you just let yourself get swept up in it all. It was out of your control.

SOPHIE: No. Not at all. It was my choice. Always.

MOHR: The court will see...

SOPHIE: The court should see that what we did, we did together. I am just as guilty as he is.

MOHR: These reckless, egotistical actions. These are not the actions of a calm, sensible young woman like you, are they? In a moment of weakness, you were taken in...

SOPHIE: I knew what I was doing. Always.

MOHR: You made a terrible mistake.

SOPHIE: No, I didn't. I would do it again.

MOHR: Surely, now that you are here, now you know the consequences...

SOPHIE: I would do it again. Whatever happens. Whatever the consequences.

MOHR: You don't need to protect him. You don't need to protect any of them. You just need to accept your mistake, ask for forgiveness and promise to...

SOPHIE: The Nazis think that conscience is a myth, don't they? You want me to abandon everything I know is right for the sake of what? Power, violence and victory? My conscience is mine. You can take everything else from me, you can't take that.

MOHR: Then think of your parents. To lose a son is bad enough, you want them to lose a daughter too? All you have to do, all you have to say...

SOPHIE: I'll make no bargain with Nazis.

MOHR: I am trying to save your life. Can't you see that? All you need to do is write the truth down here in black and white.

SOPHIE: I won't tell your lies for you. I won't betray my brother. I won't betray my beliefs.

MOHR: Sophie. I am offering you your life.

SOPHIE: I reject it.

SCENE THIRTEEN

Sophie's cell.

MOHR enters.

He hands SOPHIE her indictment.

She tries to read it, but her hands shake.

He takes it and reads it, as he reads it she finds her resolve again.

MOHR: The People's Court sentence...

SOPHIE: Is it death?

MOHR: Yes.

SOPHIE: What's the charge?

MOHR: High treason.

A moment.

SOPHIE: Good.

He looks at her but doesn't ask what she means.

SOPHIE: I am just as guilty as Hans, I should get the same punishment.

MOHR: ...

SOPHIE: What's one life? One death? Among so many.

MOHR: It's yours.

SOPHIE: Will they hang me, do you think?

MOHR: How can you ask a question like that?

SOPHIE: Will they hang me in public for my parents to see?

MOHR: No. It will be by guillotine.

SOPHIE: Guillotine?

MOHR: Yes.

SOPHIE: Oh.

MOHR: They want it done quickly. Quietly. You were right, you have worried them.

SOPHIE: When you offered me my life. It was never yours to give.

MOHR: I came in to tell you to write your letters to your parents. You will not get time later.

SOPHIE: Yes.

SOPHIE has already written some.

SOPHIE: For my parents. My sister. And my friend Fritz. You will give them to them?

MOHR: Yes.

She looks at the letters, and she is about to cry.

She doesn't cry.

She gives them to MOHR.

MOHR tries to give a few comforting words but they fail him.

SOPHIE is calm and resolved again.

She prepares herself.

SOPHIE exits.

MOHR is shaken.

MOHR exits.

SCENE FOURTEEN

Several months later.

GISELA sits in her cell.

MOHR enters. He has been promoted thanks to his success in this case but is tired and has lost some of his assurance.

MOHR: Time to go.

GISELA doesn't say anything.

MOHR: Gisela. It is your turn again. Are you ready to take the stand?

GISELA: No.

MOHR: It is OK. You just need to say what we discussed.

GISELA: I can't do it.

MOHR: What? Why not?

GISELA: How many people have to die? When does it stop?

MOHR: That is out of our control. You and me.

GISELA: Is it? Then what do you need me for? You don't need my "testimony". I won't do it anymore.

MOHR: Come on, stop being silly. Of course we need you.

GISELA: What for? These trials are a fake. You know how it ends already. Death, death and more death.

MOHR: It will help our people to see something like this, help them stay strong. Strong enough to win. It looks better, of course it looks better, to have someone who has done the right thing like you have, Gisela, to denounce the others who haven't. You have an important role to play. Come on, Gisela, your people need you.

GISELA: I don't denounce anyone, I won't, I don't want to play a role.

MOHR: It's a bit late for that. Come on, let's go.

GISELA: Get away from me.

MOHR: You won't bring them back, you know. Hans. Sophie.

GISELA: They... I wasn't... That wasn't me.

MOHR: No, no. There was not much you could do for them. Neither could I, really, but...

GISELA: Please. Please I don't want to. I want to take it back. I have sat here and seen the others, one by one...

MOHR: What?

GISELA: I never thought, I couldn't see my part in it before. In all of it. It wasn't me doing it. But now, here, sitting here, I can't see anything else. I don't want it on my conscience.

MOHR: There's that word again. It seems to seep in. Seeping in and up and around you until it's everywhere.

SCENE FIFTEEN

1960s.

For her lecture, GISELA has gathered her papers together.

GISELA: Sophie.

In the days after you died.

The posters went up.

Denouncing you as traitors and outsiders.

At the university they held a rally, and thousands of students cheered the janitor who turned you in.

They thought they had silenced you.

MOHR enters.

He switches on the radio.

A foreign news broadcast.

GISELA: But famous Germans in exile celebrated you.

RADIO: Good, splendid young people! You shall not have died in vain. You shall not be forgotten. The Nazis have raised monuments to indecent thugs and common killers in Germany. But the German Revolution, the real revolution will tear them down and, in their place, will memorialise you, who, at the time when Germany and Europe were still enveloped in the dark of night, knew and publicly declared "A new faith in freedom and honour is dawning."

MOHR switches off radio.

GISELA: Allied planes dropped your leaflets all over Germany.

MOHR picks up a leaflet and looks at it.

GISELA: After the war Mohr wrote to your father.

MOHR takes out a letter. He appears as if he is now under questioning.

MOHR: Dear Lord Mayor, Sir,

I admired your daughter very much.

Her letters didn't get to you. It was orders. If they were posted they could be used as propaganda. I didn't agree, really. I tried to help your daughter. I really did. My transfer to the Gestapo before the war was worst thing to ever happen to me and my family. Really, please believe me, it was not because I wanted to. But I always tried to do my duty. People were lucky to get me as their agent. I hope you won't think I'm exaggerating when I say I spared many people the worst. I could keep on listing people I helped, if only I could just remember their names...

GISELA: My punishment, has been to live.

I give these talks. To warn people of the danger.

I just want to make it up. I want to take it back.

Please.

...

Sophie. The free, peaceful democratic country you

spoke out for, stood up for,

We live in it now.

A few days after you died, a piece of graffiti appeared at the University:

"You can break the body but not the spirit,

Scholl lives."

THE END

STORM LANTERN QUESTIONS FOR STUDENTS

1. Why do you think Sophie and Hans chose the university as a place to drop the leaflets?

2. Why do you think the character of Hans Scholl is mentioned but never seen in the play?

3. What are the differences between the characters of Sophie and Gisela? How are these contrasts demonstrated in the play?

4. What choices have the characters made that have led them to the point where we find them at the beginning of the play? And what choices do they have within the play?

5. What do you think Sophie wants to achieve when she takes the full responsibility onto herself?

6. Can you identify the times Mohr attempts to evade or deflect responsibility for his actions or his role in events?

7. What is propaganda? How is it used as a way of influencing people? How can it be used as a system of control?

8. Why do you think Strange Town chose this particular story to turn into a play?

9. What pictures or images do you see in your head when you read the play? Were these different from what you saw when/ if you saw the play performed? How might you choose to stage your ideas?

10. Before reading the script or seeing the play how much did you know about the story of Sophie & Hans Scholl and the White Rose movement?

11. If Sophie is an example of courage and principle, can you think of any other examples of these qualities from history, stories or real life? How would you approach writing or acting these stories?

12. Can stories from history tell us things about ourselves and help us explore the world we live in today?

ALSO AVAILABLE FROM SALAMANDER STREET

All Salamander Street plays can be bought in bulk at a discount for performance or study. Contact info@salamanderstreet.com to enquire about performance licenses.

KINDNESS: A LEGACY OF THE HOLOCAUST
by Cate Hollis & Mark Wheeller
ISBN: 9781914228186

A verbatim play based on the testimony of Hungarian Holocaust survivor Susan Pollack OBE, aged only thirteen when she was sent to the notorious Auschwitz-Birkenau in the summer of 1944.

INDIGO GIANT by Ben Musgrave
ISBN: 9781738429332

A haunting drama by award-winning playwright Ben Musgrave, inspired by Dinabandhu Mitra's trail-blazing *Indigo Mirror*, a play that shook colonial India. Songs in English and Bangla by Leesa Gazi.

LOVE BITES by Sam Siggs
ISBN: 9781914228391

A park bench, school playground, a cafe, swimming pool flumes, a bar, a wind farm, a flat - all settings for this collection of short plays about falling in love. For performers aged 14-16.

BALISONG by Jennifer Adam
ISBN: 9781914228377

A play written for schools as part of the No Knives Better Lives Programme, Balisong is a story about Finlay Richards.

PLACEHOLDER by Catherine Bisset
ISBN: 9781914228919

Profoundly thought-provoking, this solo play about the historical actor-singer of colour known as 'Minette' offers an exploration of the complex racial and social dynamics of what would become the first independent nation in the Caribbean.